For Tom and Claire

First published 2008 by Walker Books Ltd
87 Vauxhall Walk, London SE11 5HJ

2 4 6 8 10 9 7 5 3 1

This book has been typeset in Gill Sans MT Schoolbook.

Printed in China.

British Library Cataloguing in Publication Data:
a catalogue record for this book is available
from the British Library.

ISBN 978-1-4063-0906-5

www.walkerbooks.co.uk

Tilly and
her friends
all live
together in
a little yellow
house...

Hello
Tilly

Polly Dunbar

WALKER BOOKS
AND SUBSIDIARIES
LONDON • BOSTON • SYDNEY • AUCKLAND

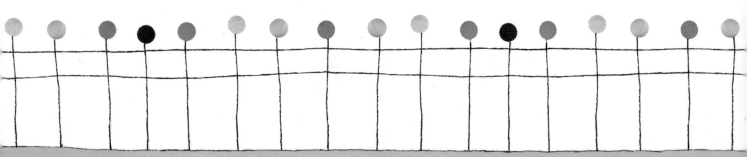

Tilly
was sitting
quietly.

She was
reading her
favourite
story.

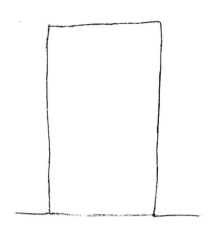

"Hello, Tilly,"
said Tiptoe.
"Will you play
with me?"

Tilly played her trumpet.

Tiptoe banged his drum.

ROOTY-TOOT-TOOT!

BOOM! BOOM!

Hector
joined in.
He danced the
wiggly-woo!

"Quick!"

said Doodle.

"There's a feast!"

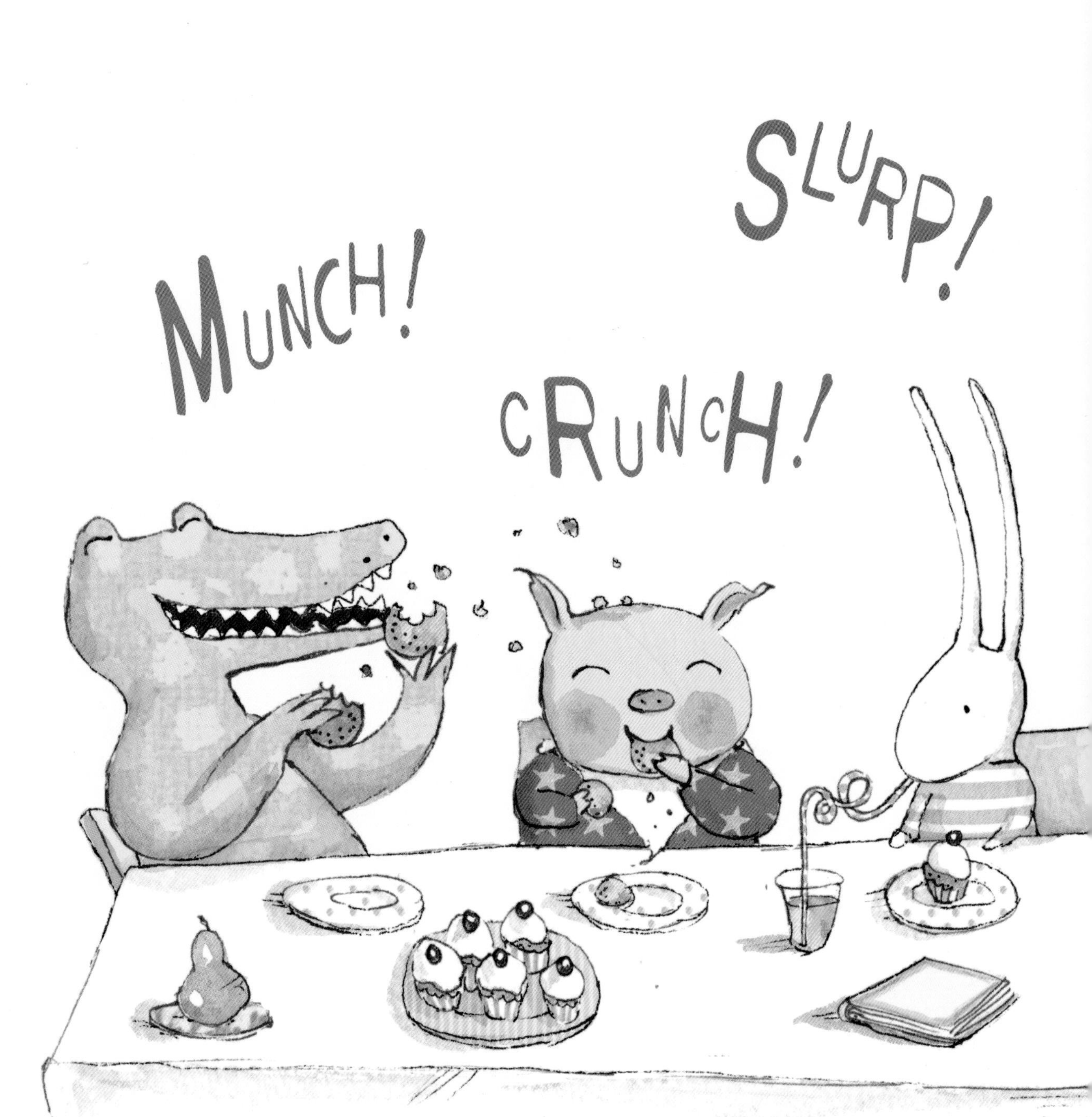
MUNCH!
CRUNCH!
SLURP!

Mmmm...?

"Surprise, everyone!" said Pru.

"It's **ME!**"

"Don't I look

LOVELY!"

"We must all do the pretty-prance,"

said Pru. "Follow me!"

WHuMP!! BuMP! WHOOPs!

"Hello, everyone!" said Tumpty.

"Come for a ride!"

What a lot of fun!

BOOM!
BOOM! BOOM!

Too much fun!

"Now
I think it's time
for a story,"
said Tilly.

"There were
six best friends,"
Tilly began,
"and they
all lived together
in a little
yellow house..."

The End